EXPLORERS AND COLONIZATION™

JACQUES CARTIER

Navigator Who Claimed Canada for France

CORONA BREZINA

ROSEN
PUBLISHING®

New York

Published in 2017 by The Rosen Publishing Group, Inc.
29 East 21st Street, New York, NY 10010

Copyright © 2017 by The Rosen Publishing Group, Inc.

First Edition

Library of Congress Cataloging-in-Publication Data

Names: Brezina, Corona, author.
Title: Jacques Cartier: Navigator Who Claimed Canada for France / Corona Brezina.
Description: First edition. | New York : Rosen Publishing, [2017] | Series:
 Spotlight on explorers and colonization | Includes bibliographical
 references and index.
Identifiers: LCCN 2016018583| ISBN 9781508172086 (library bound) | ISBN
 9781508172062 (pbk.) | ISBN 9781508172079 (6-pack)
Subjects: LCSH: Explorers—America—Biography—Juvenile literature. |
 Explorers—France—Biography—Juvenile literature. | Canada—Discovery and
 exploration—French—Juvenile literature. | Canada—History—To 1763 (New
 France)—Juvenile literature.
Classification: LCC E133.C3 B74 2016 | DDC 910.92 [B] —dc23
LC record available at https://lccn.loc.gov/2016018583

Manufactured in China

CONTENTS

JACQUES CARTIER, DISCOVERER OF CANADA

On August 13, 1535, the explorer Jacques Cartier prepared to enter the mouth of the St. Lawrence River. Native Americans had told him fantastical stories about the river and the lands beyond, including the mythical Kingdom of Saguenay. Cartier later wrote down the natives' description, "that farther up, the water became fresh, and that one could make one's way so far up the river that they had never heard of anyone reaching the end of it."

Cartier had been sent to the New World to seek treasure and a water passage leading to

China and the East. Francis I, king of France, hoped that exploration and colonization of the New World would bring France great riches.

Cartier found neither gold nor the Northwest Passage, but today he is remembered as the first European to travel the St. Lawrence River. Many locations and geological features still bear the names Cartier gave them on his maps, including Canada itself.

CARTIER'S EARLY LIFE

Jacques Cartier was born in Saint-Malo, France, in 1491. Saint-Malo is a small seaport in the province of Brittany in northwestern France. Cartier came from a respected seafaring family. Little is known about his early life and education. He probably started out working as a ship's boy at a young age, rising to become a sailor and then an officer. He would have studied astronomy, mathematics, navigation, and cartography. Cartography, or mapmaking, was a valuable skill in an age when explorers were being sent out to discover and map new lands.

In 1519, Cartier married Marie Katherine de Granches, the daughter of an important

JACQUES CARTIER.

A monument to Cartier stands in his hometown of Saint-Malo in Brittany, France. During his lifetime, he was highly respected by the townspeople.

official in Saint-Malo. The couple never had any children. In an age when social standing greatly influenced a person's opportunities for success, this marriage would have increased Cartier's status. Marriage documents describe Cartier as a "master pilot," which would have been equivalent to the position of first mate on a ship.

SAILING TO AMERICA

Cartier is believed to have sailed to the New World during his early career. He probably studied at Dieppe, home of France's leading school of navigation and cartography and the adopted hometown of the Italian explorer Giovanni da Verrazzano. According to some accounts, Cartier accompanied Verrazzano during his expedition to the North American coast. Verrazzano's ship reached present-day North Carolina in January 1524 and spent the next three months exploring the east coast, all the way up to Newfoundland.

Cartier may also have traveled to Brazil. He spoke Portuguese and implied in a letter

Giovanni da Verrazzano's exploration of the Atlantic coastline of North America during the early sixteenth century significantly expanded European understanding of the geography of the New World.

that he was familiar with Brazilian crops. He almost certainly sailed the North Atlantic Ocean, probably as part of Breton fishing fleets. A letter of recommendation to Francis I mentioned that he had been to both Newfoundland and Brazil. Regardless of his specific voyages, Cartier was one of France's leading navigators and cartographers on the eve of his commission to explore the New World.

SETTING OUT FOR THE "NEW LANDS"

In March 1534, King Francis I commissioned Cartier to lead a voyage of discovery to the New World. Spanish explorers had found gold and established an empire in South America, and Francis hoped that his explorers would make discoveries that would make France an imperial power. Cartier's official mandate was to search for lands that would yield gold and other riches. The other objective of the voyage was to search for the fabled Northwest Passage, which would give France a trade route to China.

Very little was known about the area Cartier was sent to explore. A document

Cartier and his men waited impatiently for the ice pack around Newfoundland to clear and allow the ships to pass. Previous French explorers had failed to reach the continent's interior.

from the time directed that he explore the "Bay of Castles," for example, but the so-called bay was really just a strait.

Cartier departed France on April 20, 1534. He set sail with two ships, each with a crew of thirty men. The expedition benefitted from favorable weather and reached Newfoundland twenty days later, but ice pack prevented the ships from making landfall.

CARTIER'S FIRST VOYAGE

On June 9, Cartier's ships sailed through the Strait of Belle Isle into the Gulf of St. Lawrence. During the journey, he had encountered many French fishing vessels. By June 15, their westward course had taken them into areas that had not been explored by Europeans. Cartier gave names to the islands and geological features, many of them the names of Catholic saints.

Cartier found the northern islands to be barren and forbidding, but he began to observe fertile soil further inland as he traveled south. His men made four expeditions into Prince Edward Island, which Cartier believed

The Strait of Belle Isle is the 90-mile- (145 km) long waterway separating Newfoundland from mainland Canada. It had never been accurately mapped by Europeans before Cartier's exploration.

was part of the mainland. In early July, while exploring the coast of present-day Canada, Cartier's men became the first Frenchmen to trade goods with Native Americans—probably Micmacs. His crew offered iron goods, such as knives and hatchets, in exchange for furs. Although Cartier had fired a warning shot with a cannon upon first glimpsing the Native American canoes, the interactions between the two groups were peaceful.

"LONG LIVE THE KING OF FRANCE"

As Cartier sailed past the Gaspé peninsula in present-day Canada, a storm forced the ships to shelter in a bay. There, Cartier encountered members of an Iroquois tribe fishing. Cartier offered them some trinkets as gifts and received a warm welcome. In records, he described how they dressed and raised crops.

Once ashore, however, Cartier's men claimed possession of the land for France on July 24 by erecting a thirty-foot (nine-meter) cross. A plaque proclaimed, "Long live the King of France." The Iroquois chief, Donnaconna, protested. Cartier appeased

Cartier glimpsed the entrance to the St. Lawrence River during his first voyage, but he began to explore it only upon returning to Canada on his second expedition.

him by claiming that it was just an insignificant marker.

Cartier also took two of Donnaconna's sons back to France on his return voyage. According to some accounts, Donnaconna allowed this as a goodwill gesture. According to others, the two boys were captives. As the ships sailed northward past Anticosti Island, Cartier saw a passage of open water toward the northwest, but the weather would not allow for further exploration.

HEADING HOME

The ships began their return voyage to France in August. Cartier's officers agreed that they did not want to risk being stranded in the wild through the winter.

Cartier had frequently heard Native Americans speak the word *kanata*, meaning "settlement." Believing that it described the land itself, Cartier used the word in his writings and maps. This misunderstanding was the origin of the name Canada.

Francis I considered Cartier's voyage promising enough that he approved a second expedition almost immediately. The king commissioned him to explore the

This romanticized nineteenth-century landscape painting depicts Cartier and his crew encountering Native Americans as they begin exploration of the St. Lawrence River.

passage leading northwest in the hope that it would lead to China and yield discoveries of gold and other precious minerals. The Iroquois boys, Domagaya and Taignoagny, had learned to speak some French. They told of a mighty river flowing inward that lead to the Kingdom of Saguenay, a land of great riches. Cartier's second expedition was scheduled to depart in May 1535.

CARTIER'S SHIPS AND CREW

Cartier led three ships (rather than the two of his first voyage) and commanded about 110 men on his second expedition. The ships were *La Grande Hermine* (The Great Stoat), which was twice the size of either ship from his previous expedition, as well as *La Petite Hermine* (The Lesser Stoat) and the smaller *L'Émérillon* (The Merlin), which was a suitable size for inland exploration. The ships carried adequate provisions and supplies for a fifteen-month voyage—Cartier planned to winter over in the New World.

Most of the men were experienced seamen from Cartier's hometown of Saint-Malo, and a

41

La Grande Hermine

MARSHALL ISLANDS

C272. (12-2)   ©2008

Cartier's ship *La Grande Hermine* was a carrack, a type of large, oceangoing sailing ship with three or four masts that was used by many explorers during the Age of Discovery.

dozen were his relatives. Domagaya and Taignoagny were returning home, as Cartier had promised Donnaconna. They would also serve as guides and sources of information.

After beginning the journey, the three ships experienced a month of tempests and became separated from each other. They met up in late July and entered the Gulf of St. Lawrence in early September.

RETURN TO CANADA

The Gulf of St. Lawrence led into the vast St. Lawrence River, which is today known to be the major waterway in the region. Cartier's ships were now returning to Iroquois territory. They sailed inward for about five hundred miles (eight hundred kilometers) and marveled at the beluga whales, game, and other wildlife. During the trip, the men encountered groups of Iroquois who recognized Domagaya and Taignoagny. When the ships neared the boys' home village of Stadacona, Donnaconna met them and was reunited with his sons. They held a celebration and the chief welcomed the French back to his land. However, he did not invite them into the village.

An artist's rendering shows Cartier's ships at the site of present-day Quebec. Natives told him that *kebec* meant "where the river narrows" in their language.

Cartier anchored his two larger ships in a harbor close to Stadacona. He ordered some of his men to prepare for the upcoming winter at the site of present-day Quebec City. Meanwhile, he continued inland exploration up the St. Lawrence River.

EXPLORING THE ST. LAWRENCE RIVER

Cartier planned to travel further up the St. Lawrence to a larger Native American settlement called Hochelaga. The Iroquois there belonged to a different tribe from Donnaconna, and he did not want the French to make an alliance with his rivals. He tried to persuade Cartier that the river wasn't worth exploring, and Domagaya and Taignoagny refused to serve as guides. The day before Cartier planned to leave, three natives dressed in costume as devils warned them that they would meet their doom if they continued.

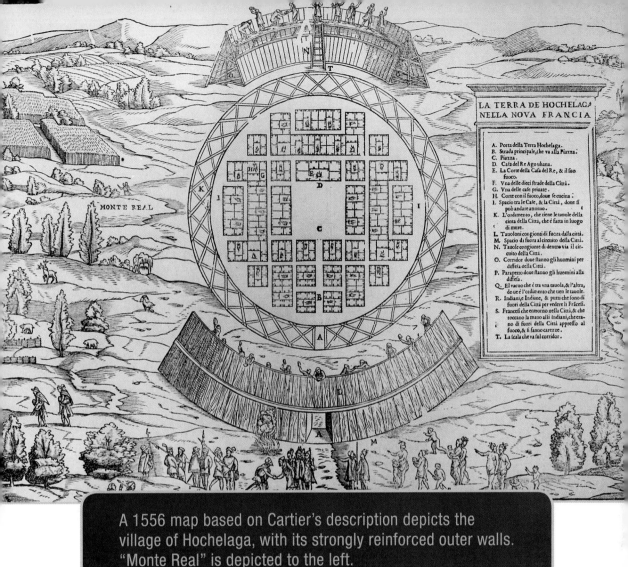

LA TERRA DE HOCHELAGA
NELLA NOVA FRANCIA

A. Porta della Terra Hochelaga.
B. Strada principale, che va alla Piazza.
C. Piazza.
D. Casa del Re Agouhanna.
E. La Corte della Casa del Re, & il suo fuoco.
F. Vna delle dieci strade della Città.
G. Vna delle case priuate.
H. Corte con il fuoco, doue se cucina.
I. Spacio tra le Case, & la Città, doue si può andare attorno.
K. L'ordimento, che tiene le tauole della cinta della Città, che è fatta in luogo di mure.
L. Tauoloni congionti di fuora dalla città.
M. Spacio di fuora al circuito della Città.
N. Tauole congionte di dentro via il circuito della Città.
O. Corridor doue stanno gli huomini per diffesa della Città.
P. Parapetto doue stanno gli huomini alla diffesa.
Q. El vacuo che è tra vna tauola, & l'altra, do ue è l'ordimento che tien le tauole.
R. Indiani, e Indiane, & putti che sono di fuori della Città per vedere li Francesi.
S. Francesi che entrorno nella Città, & che toccano la mano alli Indiani, che erano di fuori della Città appresso al fuoco, & si fanno carezze.
T. La scala che va sul corridor.

MONTE REAL

A 1556 map based on Cartier's description depicts the village of Hochelaga, with its strongly reinforced outer walls. "Monte Real" is depicted to the left.

Nevertheless, *L'Émérillon* sailed the next day. Cartier's party included his officers and about half of the sailors.

Cartier was impressed by the rich variety of wildlife along the banks. They also met many friendly natives as they traveled inland.

The river gradually became more difficult to navigate, however. Cartier decided to continue onward in longboats, leaving some men behind with *L'Émérillon.* Natives indicated that he could reach Hochelaga in three day's time.

Hochelaga was much larger than Stadacona. Fifty large houses, each containing many spacious rooms, were protected by extensive fortifications. A thousand people welcomed Cartier and his men, believing that they were miracle workers. Cartier exchanged knives and trinkets for fish and cornbread.

The island settlement is the site of present-day Montreal. Cartier explored a nearby mountain that he named Mont-Royal. He could see that impassable rapids lay ahead on the St. Lawrence River. The Iroquois at Hochelaga indicated that a river to the north led to the Saguenay Kingdom, where gold and silver could be found.

Cartier spent only a day at Hochelaga before returning in the longboats to

Cartier arrived at Hochelaga on foot, guided across trails by three natives. Here, he is depicted greeting one of the leaders of the town.

L'Émérillon. The expedition reached Stadacona on October 11. Meanwhile, the men left behind had erected a fort, which they worked to strengthen before winter. Relations with Donnaconna's tribe had grown tense. The chief invited Cartier to his village upon his return, but the Iroquois and French remained suspicious of each other.

THE LONG, CRUEL WINTER

The French were unprepared for the New World's harsh winter. By mid-November 1535, Cartier's ships were frozen into the river. Their provisions froze, fresh food ran low, and the men grew weak. Most came to suffer from a disease called scurvy. Twenty-five men died. Despite tense relations between the French and Iroquois, Domagaya taught the French how to brew a remedy from a conifer tree. The surviving crewmembers quickly recovered. The Iroquois also introduced the French to tobacco, which they believed to have healthful properties.

Cartier reported on Canada's abundant natural resources to the king of France. Eventually, the fur trade would prove highly profitable to the French in Canada.

Donnaconna had told Cartier many tales about the riches of Saguenay. Before setting sail in the spring, Cartier forcibly abducted Donnaconna so he could personally describe this land to the king of France. His presence as an onboard hostage would also guarantee the ships' safe passage. Cartier also seized Domagaya, Taignoagny, and several others, claiming that they would be returned to their land in a year. The ships reached Saint-Malo on July 15, 1536.

A NEW MANDATE

Cartier and his men returned to a country on the brink of war with Spain. Cartier was unable to present his findings to the court for a year. Further exploration of the New World was postponed. Meanwhile, Cartier was given *La Grande Hermine* for his services and he sailed as a privateer, plundering Spanish and Portuguese ships. Donnaconna and all but one of the Native Americans died. The war ended in 1538.

Francis I did not authorize a new expedition to Canada until 1540. This time, Cartier was under the command of Jean Francois de la Rocque, Lord of Roberval. Roberval was given the mandate of establishing towns and forts—a royal

Losten de Poix

Roberval was born into an old and distinguished family, but he had managed his finances badly and hoped to make his fortune in Canada.

colony. Despite his lack of sailing experience, Roberval was a nobleman, and he would be the governor of French lands in the New World.

Cartier commanded five ships, which carried livestock and supplies for two years. When Roberval had difficulty recruiting crewmembers, Cartier had to take on notorious convicts and women.

THE COLONY OF CHARLESBOURG ROYAL

Cartier sailed in May 1541. Roberval was to follow with four ships and his men, which included the soldiers attached to the venture, after further preparation. In the meantime, Cartier had been charged with continuing his exploration and finding the Kingdom of Saguenay. Cartier's third expedition is less well documented than his first two voyages.

After reaching Stadacona in August, Cartier told the Iroquois that Donnaconna had died and the others had chosen to stay in France. The ships continued about 8 more miles (13 km) up the St. Lawrence River. Cartier anchored at a site now known

Today a suburb of Quebec City, Cap Rouge was the site of Cartier's settlement of Charlesbourg Royal. Roberval renamed the colony France-Roy when he arrived.

as Cap Rouge, on the Chaudière River, which branched southward off of the St. Lawrence River.

There, Cartier established a settlement called Charlesbourg Royal. The men constructed two forts, one atop a cliff overlooking the river and the other at its foot. They also began cultivating crops and mining for gold and other minerals.

UPRIVER EXPLORATION

On September 7, Cartier left with a small number of men to explore the St. Lawrence River and search for gold. He planned to lead a larger follow-up expedition in the spring. Cartier left command of Charlesbourg Royal in the hands of his brother-in-law, Viscount Beaupré.

During his previous expedition, he had visited the village of Achelacy. Cartier returned to the village and renewed friendly relations with the chief, leaving two French boys in his care so that they could learn the Iroquois language and culture. Future French settlers would continue to use this system for teaching interpreters.

Leading cartographers of the day added Cartier's discoveries to their maps. This 1546 world map includes details of the Gulf of St. Lawrence and the St. Lawrence River.

Cartier proceeded upriver to the rapids that he had glimpsed when he had visited Hochelaga. This time, however, he made no record of visiting Hochelaga. Other natives living in the area told him that another set of rapids further up the river was even more difficult to navigate and that Saguenay lay beyond. Cartier abandoned exploration and turned back.

A WINTER UNDER SIEGE

On the return trip down the St. Lawrence River, Cartier discovered that Achelacy was nearly deserted. He heard that several tribes were banding together to mount an attack on the French. When the expedition returned to Charlesbourg Royal, Cartier found that the relationship between the French and the Native Americans had deteriorated. Records do not describe the specific cause of the Iroquois's hostility.

Cartier ordered his men to reinforce the defenses around the fort. The French spent much of the winter barricaded inside the walls. They suffered from scurvy once again, although they were spared the worst consequences by the Iroquois-taught

After spending a difficult year in Canada during his third expedition, Cartier recognized that the colony could not survive and resolved to return to France.

conifer preparation. The Native Americans never launched an organized attack against the French, but they did harass the settlers with raids. More than thirty colonists were killed. Provisions began to run low. In June 1542, Cartier resolved to abandon the colony and return to France.

A RENDEZVOUS AND A RETREAT

When he reached Newfoundland, Cartier finally met up with Roberval, who had only departed in April 1542. Cartier tried to warn Roberval that returning to Charlesbourg Royal would only lead to disaster. Nonetheless, Roberval ordered Cartier to turn back. Rather than obey, Cartier sailed for France under cover of night.

Roberval continued onward and established his own settlement, France-Roy, near Charlesbourg Royal. His men erected a fort and several surrounding buildings. When winter came, however, the settlers suffered badly from scurvy and fifty died. The survivors were reduced to near starvation rations. Those who complained

An early sixteenth-century map of the east coast of North America incorporates contributions from Cartier's explorations. Cartier and his men are shown disembarking in the foreground.

were whipped or put in shackles. When spring arrived, Roberval traveled up the St. Lawrence River to seek Saguenay, but like Cartier, the rapids prevented him. Eight men drowned when one of the boats overturned. By the summer of 1843, Roberval decided to give up on the attempt to colonize the New World.

CARTIER'S LATER LIFE

Cartier brought back barrels full of what he believed to be gold and diamonds when he returned to France. This trove proved to be worthless iron pyrite—also called fool's gold—and quartz.

French officials ruled that Cartier had made the right decision in disobeying Roberval's orders, and he was not punished. Some records hint that Cartier may have returned to the New World in 1543 to retrieve Roberval. Cartier himself did not leave an account of the voyage, if it occurred.

Cartier settled down in his hometown of Saint-Malo. He did not undertake any more

Cartier's gold and diamonds proved to be merely iron pyrite and quartz. After his return, the phrase "diamond of Canada" came to signify something worthless but deceptively attractive.

major sea voyages, instead tending to his country estate. In 1545, he published an account of his exploration of the New World. Sailors and other explorers sometimes got together at Cartier's home to tell stories about their adventures. The people of Saint-Malo considered him one of the town's leading citizens. Jacques Cartier died in 1557.

CARTIER'S LEGACY

Cartier is remembered by history as an expert navigator who discovered the St. Lawrence River and established a French presence in the territory that would become Canada. He did attempt to befriend the Native Americans he encountered, but on some occasions, his treatment of them was disgraceful. Nonetheless, during an age when some explorers acted even more cruelly toward the natives, Cartier's attitude and actions were typical of his time.

Cartier failed to find either a passage to China or a source of gold and other riches in the New World. The 1543 to 1544 colonization attempt demonstrated that despite its natural resources, Canada was

an unfriendly territory. The Kingdom of Saguenay was only a fable.

France abandoned exploration and colonization attempts for decades. Finally, after many unsuccessful attempts, Samuel de Champlain followed Cartier's lead in exploring the region around the St. Lawrence River. In 1608, he founded Quebec City, the first French settlement to thrive in Canada, the country that owes its name to Jacques Cartier.

GLOSSARY

anchor To moor a vessel using a heavy device.

bay A body of water partially enclosed by land that is connected to an ocean or lake.

cartography The practice of making maps.

colony A territory that is under political control, often distant, of a different country.

commission A formal command or authorization.

expedition A journey undertaken by a group of people for a specific purpose.

explorer Someone who travels to unfamiliar places for the purpose of discovery.

mandate An official order to carry out a course of action.

navigator Someone who steers a ship or other means of transport, especially using maps, instruments, or the stars.

passage A journey by water from one place to another.

provisions A stock of food and other necessities provided for a journey.

rapids A fast-flowing and turbulent part of a river.

stoat A small carnivorous mammal that is a member of the weasel family.

territory A region or area of land.

tribe A social division in traditional societies, often sharing common ties such as kinship, culture, religion, and language.

trove A treasure or discovery that is important or valuable.

Canadian Museum of History
100 Laurier Street
Gatineau, QC K1A 0M8
Canada
(819) 776-7000
Website: http://www.historymuseum.ca/virtual-museum
-of-new-france/introduction
This museum, which presents exhibitions related to
history, archaeology, ethnology, and cultural studies,
features a Virtual Museum of New France that
includes information on early explorers.

Canadian Register of Historic Places (CRHP)
30 Victoria Street, 3rd Floor
Gatineau, QC J8X 0B3
Canada
Website: http://www.historicplaces.ca/en/rep-reg/place
-lieu.aspx?id=16661
The CRHP provides a source of information about all
historic places recognized for their heritage value
at the local, provincial, territorial, and national levels
throughout Canada, including Charlesbourg Royal,
the site of Cartier's settlement.

Historica Canada
2 Carlton Street, East Mezzanine
Toronto, ON M5B 1J3

Canada
(416) 506-1867
Website: https://www.historicacanada.ca
Historica Canada is the largest independent organization
    devoted to enhancing awareness of Canadian history
    and citizenship.

Mariners' Museum and Park
100 Museum Drive
Newport News, VA 23606
(757) 596-2222
Website: http://www.marinersmuseum.org
The Mariners' Museum endeavors to make a difference
    in peoples' lives by inviting them to discover their
    relationship to the sea by exploring maritime culture,
    science, and history.

Websites

Because of the changing nature of internet links, Rosen
Publishing has developed an online list of websites
related to the subject of this book. This site is updated
regularly. Please use this link to access the list:

http://www.rosenlinks.com/SEC/cart

FOR FURTHER READING

Blashfield, Jean. *Jacques Cartier in Search of the Northwest Passage.* Minneapolis, MN: Compass Point Books, 2002.

Cooke, Tim. *The Exploration of North America.* New York, NY: Gareth Stevens, 2013.

Harmon, Daniel E. *Jacques Cartier and the Exploration of Canada.* Philadelphia, PA: Chelsea House Publishers, 2001.

Johnson, Michael. *Encyclopedia of Native Tribes of North America.* Buffalo, NY: Firefly Books, 2014.

LaPlante, Walter. *Waterways of the Great Lakes.* New York, NY: Gareth Stevens Publishing, 2015.

Matthews, Rupert. *Explorer.* New York, NY: DK Books, 2012.

O'Brien, Cynthia. *Explore with Samuel de Champlain.* St. Catharines, ON: Crabtree Publishing Company, 2014.

Powell, Marie. *Explore with Jacques Cartier.* St. Catharines, ON: Crabtree Publishing Company, 2014.

Ross, Stewart. *Into the Unknown: How Great Explorers Found Their Way by Land, Sea, and Air.* Somerville, MA: Candlewick Press, 2014.

Woog, Adam. *Jacques Cartier.* Philadelphia, PA: Chelsea House Publishers, 2009.

BIBLIOGRAPHY

Axtell, James. *Beyond 1492: Encounters in Colonial North America.* New York, NY: Oxford University Press, 1992.

Canwest News Service. "Long-lost Jacques Cartier Settlement Rediscovered at Quebec City." Canada .com. August 19, 2006. http://www.canada.com /topics/news/national/story.html?id=4978e603 -f67e-4784-807d-7f3911c60829&k=27303.

Cartier, Jacques, et al. *The Voyages of Jacques Cartier.* Toronto, ON: University of Toronto Press, 1993.

Coulter, Tony. *Jacques Cartier, Samuel de Champlain, and the Explorers of Canada.* New York, NY: Chelsea House Publishers, 1993.

Cox, Caroline, and Ken Albala. *Opening Up North America: 1497–1800.* New York, NY: Facts On File, 2005.

Mariners' Museum. "Jacques Cartier." Retrieved April 11, 2016. http://ageofex.marinersmuseum.org /index.php?type=explorer&id=17.

Mattox, Jake, ed. *Explorers of the New World.* Farmington Hills, MI: Greenhaven Press, 2004.

Parks Canada. "Jacques Cartier, Explorer and Navigator." May 5, 2015. http://www.pc.gc.ca/eng /lhn-nhs/qc/cartierbrebeuf/natcul/natcul2.aspx.

INDEX

About the Author

Corona Brezina is an author who has written over a dozen young adult books for Rosen Publishing. Several of her previous books have also focused on topics related to history and world cultures, including *Celtic Mythology* and *Zheng He*. She lives in Chicago.

Photo Credits

Designer: Nicole Russo; Editor and Photo Researcher: Heather Moore Niver